Revolutions:

Night and Day

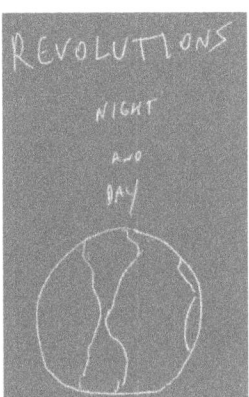

Art & Allegory

Andy Palasciano

LYMER & HART
Rainbow, California

Lymer & Hart
an imprint of Garden Oak Press
1953 Huffstatler St., Suite A
Rainbow, CA 92028
760 728-2088
gardenoakpress.com
lymerhart@gmail.com
@hartlymer

First published by Garden Oak Press on June 15, 2023.

ISBN-13: 979-8-9879532-0-4

Library of Congress Control Number: 2023939110

Printed in the United States of America

For

the Palasciano family,
the Walters family,
the Harding family,
the Ratnavira tamily,
the Hesse and Guthrie families,
the Griffin family,
Mary O'Connor,
Ashley Farrand,
Lori Cameron
and
the many Angels that God has put in my life.

Contents

Revolutions:

Night and Day

Art & Allegory

Andy Palasciano

TREE

I AM NOT A MONSTER

Rosemary,

They told you to sing
    as they cut into your brain
    and then a wire was snipped
    and you barely talked again.
        There was low television
        in your mind.
Mother and Father,
    I only want to make you proud,
    clip clip and there is someone gone
    in a car that you loved.
        Then clip in a kitchen
          you walked up the staircase
        to meet the royals.
            You were dressed
            yes
            but you were lightened.
        The water is smooth and
           light.
        Tonight there is laughter and
           swimming,
            Sweet Rosemary
             you never stopped singing.

3

Mary Wollstonecraft was in the same writing circle as
Thomas Paine.
They wrote, at the foundation of our nation,
about rights, dreaming of what the world could be.
Mary Wollstonecraft wrote *A Vindication of the Rights of
Woman*.
And Thomas Paine would write *The Rights of Man*.
Mary Wollstonecraft dreamed that women
would be equal to men
if they were given the chance to be educated.
Niceties at the time said it was impolite for women to get
educated.
Mary Wollstonecraft died from complications from giving
birth to Mary Shelley.
Mary Shelley would later write *Frankenstein*, indirectly,
because she felt like a
monster for her mother dying to give birth to her.
But this monster,
a woman educated and bright in a dim world,
was not a tragedy.
When Amanda Gorman read her poem at the inauguration
of a President,
she was a descendent of slaves,
whose rights were those of man. She was a
woman governed by love and not a monster.
The Monster of *Frankenstein* found
what this young poet found:
that love is kind and
stronger than monsters.

Mary Wollstonecraft dreamed of a land where women weren't just quaint and beautiful, but educated and bright. Women were in their sewing rooms and keeping proper. Thoughts had grown stale in these sewing and powder rooms. Sitting on a couch, Mary felt it was time for a change and got up and stepped out of the powder room in an impolite way. It was dark at the time and there were no stars. She heard a voice sing, "And don't be afraid of the dark." Gaining courage, she picked up a torch at the castle door. She made her way in the blackening twilight. She felt alone and heard the same voice say, "You'll never walk alone." Mary gained courage and walked down the road of leafless trees. She saw a monster ahead. It was walking toward her. Mary saw a baby lying in a crib on the path. She picked up the baby and held it. The monster came closer. Suddenly, she heard the voice of many women in the thicket. They sang an other-worldly song. Mary knew from the voices that the monster would eat the baby if she did not offer herself up for a meal. She put the baby down with the torch nearby so she would be found. And Mary stood with the thousand female voices and walked into the darkness.

In the dark there is a riddle.
Who is the darkness?
Is it a space between light?
Or is it the end of a day of
revolutions?
Is the darkness a scream or a
shout whistling through trees?
Is the darkness,
rumored of horrors,
just the blanket of
time?
Where galaxies dream?
Or is the darkness in our hearts?
Where lives gluttony and guile?
Creation calls to the deer in the night.
And the eyes glow like orbs,
and the river continues to flow.

Whittling with a stick
he was sitting right next to me.
There was a parlance of time,
   a fold of crease before the barn
      and the moonlight,
     a ripple in the lake
  You were with me,
     were you not?

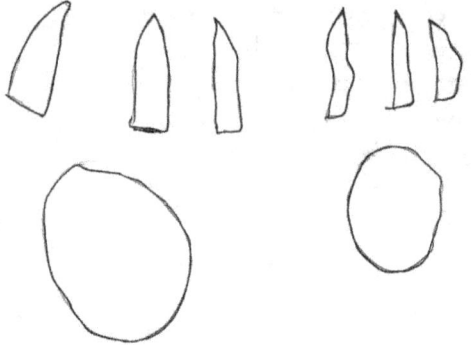

Steaming drops of green pain ooze
down bare cliff,
writhing under jade moonlight
we do drift,
two primal, moss laden energies—
one,
yet when shall we know
Holy light of sun?
The eyes of the dragon escape
its steamed breath,
while tears of a mystic
fall to their death,
who is to know what
pleasures remain unseen?
For now may we drift
in tidepools of green.

The
Starry Ever

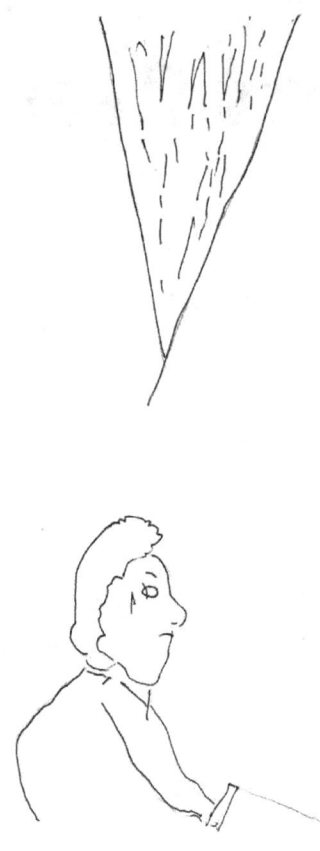

Reginald pushed his cart under
The Starry Ever. The villagers called him
The Village Fool. Reginald had no
home and talked to himself, but no
one listened to him. Reginald thought
The Starry Ever was so far away
but The Starry Ever heard every
word that Reginald said and answered
each word.

Sometimes Reginald didn't like
what The Starry Ever told him. There
were words like "No," and "Not now."
When Reginald indirectly asked for
something through his cry and was
told, "Not now," Reginald said many
words but the heart of the words,
which no one could decipher
but The Starry Ever, was saying, "You
 always say 'no,' and you put me
working toward it, you promised."
And The Starry Ever said,
"I said, 'Not right now,' not 'No'."

The people of the town
thought Regianld talked to no
one and was like a piece of
dust in the vacuum of space.
And that no one cared where
that dust landed. But little
did they know that The Starry
Ever cared about nothing more
than where this "Village Fool,"
as they called him, was going
to lay down his head to
rest for the night.

There was a thatch
house on the banks of the
river. Reginald walked by along
the river but was spoken to,
something that hadn't happened in
some time, by the man who owned
the thatch house. He said,
"Come and stay in my guest
house. There is room for you."

That night Reginald made his
soft bed with blankets and went outside
to the fire by the riverside and warmed
himself. In that moment, as he looked
up to The Starry Ever, he realized
it wasn't so far away and that
in that Ever was one loving person.
It was the first time he called
into The Starry Ever, "Lord,"
that is to say, Daddy.

There is a mist
of catacombs, a relentless
sea of turquoise caves.
We have a lantern on
our raft and there
are bats about us.
We are heading toward
a hollow, but are
traveling toward the
cave opening where
there is a lake in
the lit forest and
there is a breeze on the water.
We emerged from
the opening of the cave and
were greeted by crickets and cicadas.
Evening fast approached and we
rested upon the shore. We
didn't need to be covered by
the cave anymore.

TOTO, I DON'T THINK WE'RE IN KANSAS ANYMORE

A Window
to the
World

The cold moot horns of bicycles
in the sewer dungeon-like basements
the crying flowers of winter's majesty

The gray
window
by the bay

Blight
the candle
and whisper

The New
Fangled
Day

Spangled
children
unwrapped
and
bouncing
on The
blanket
of
Wilbur

THE LOLLIPOP
GUILD

Mika's hue of chestnut
found me stumbling
around like a star's lusk
God swung the revolving door
And I met her crying
on the floor

.

THE LOLLIPOP KID

FOLLOW THE YELLOW BRICK ROAD

The Lord led me and Samantha to a giant cactus
The cactus was bulbous
It cupped in the middle and went outward high
its arms protecting the white center
In the middle of the cup lay kittens
barely visible from the outside
But through a small shaft of sunlight
a gray and white mane could be seen
I held Samantha's body through the sunlight
high where the arms spread out
so she could see the nest of kittens
She was amazed
The Lord's guidance is always amazing

BUT I
GUESS I'M ALREADY THERE

The white helicopter
          Seeds flutter all around
The summer trees are
snowing. To the right
          a tree draped in brown
Its hair catching sunflakes
          They are at your feet
                    God's Royalty

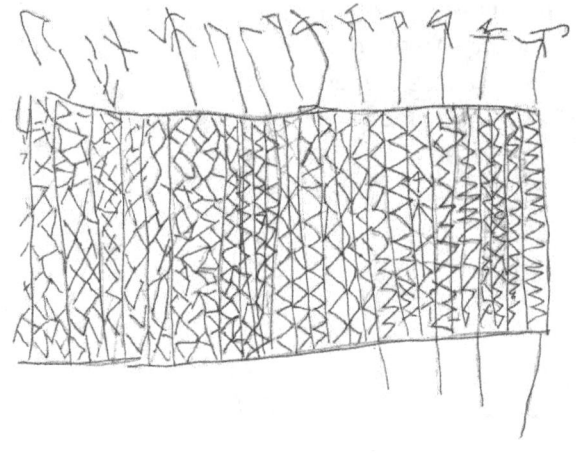

There is ancient farm equipment
down at the ancient fence post.
   That lady knew Everett was an old farm hand
by the way Everett put his hands in his front pockets
         of his jeans.
   Everett never apologized.
   Unchecked by the check lines
            the mules are running free
            some with barbed wire around their neck.
   They are going to see the Chief.
   The planes fly so high in the air
            so big to hear.
   The gentle birds don't like the wild birds
            when they get in that giant coup
            beneath the playhouse.
   Why are the wild birds afraid of the gentle birds?
   The sound is like a bee hive.
   Why did they cut that bull's horns off?
   "I told them not to cut them off.
   All the other bulls would get after him."
   The Chief wanted me to keep Old Shep.
   The Chief will always be on your side.

What if you are not falling?
But you have just left your nest
and are about to catch
the air with your wing
and before you hit the ground
you fly parallel to it
and up out of the canyon, and into the sky?

.

3/30/16

the common is a blue dream
but it can be bright

       when God is the dreamer
       and we
       the dream

       Two-year-old Tova tugged the blanket
       loose from the sky
       and held an entire kingdom
       in her plural eye

THE SCARECROW

Christ brought
a light

and with a
gentle might

drove His staff
into the ground

and reclaimed
the night.

I put my head
into a stoic bowl

And when I pulled
it out and saw
my reflection
I thought I had
a heroic soul

But drowning
doesn't make
a man a hero

And God cracked
the bowl

and left me
swimming for
The Kingdom
of Zero

I took my torch
  and went looking for
  The Christian Underground

      And in the cave there
      was a giant lantern ablaze
      warming the snow that

      When I looked out the other
      side there was a daylight
      with ice-skating children

      And the moccasin flower
      was weeping
      and the falling pollen
      was sleeping

The fool swam with the ducks
at night

and had a belligerent dream
of light.

There was
a lion
of orange

and white

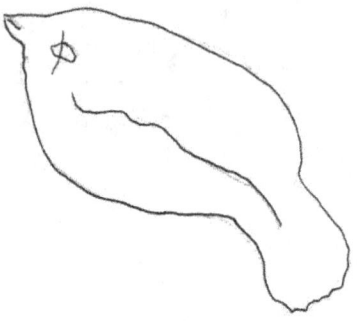

The Slug crept into our
hearts from the light.
It asked a question:
 "You blame me for your not being
 able to touch anything now. But
 should you blame yourself?
 When you had the chance, before me,
 were you like Thoreau, who gazed
 through and played in flowers, smelling
 the like? Even though others looked
 at him with disapproval? Can you
 blame the others' disapproval? Or
 should you blame your own pride?
 So don't look at me. Eternal
 lessons are branded on the
 heart through fear. May I, the
 Slug, be the seal you see
 when the mist of the rain relents
 and you dance toward a new spring.
  And you creep, slowly, back
  toward the light."

.

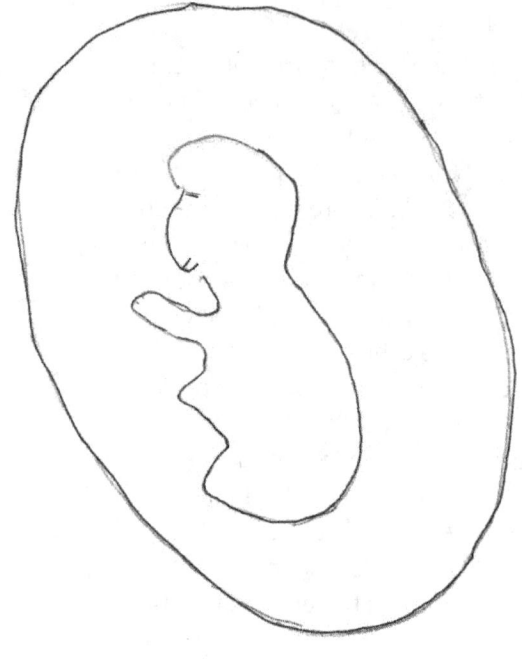

It has been tough living outside the womb. There was a cord I was plugged into. Now I am living unplugged and I feel uncharged. I cry but it is a lie. I tell my cord of old that I need food. I tug for sustenance. But my cord is no longer connected. I am free. But freedom is not terrible. I am free but I do not need to leech off the neck of my mother. I am free to live and discover. I was never disconnected. I was only given tears in my eyes so my eyes might be uncovered.

And now, as a man, I climbed the mountain to find what was deep within me. I looked upon who resided there. I proclaimed, "I have found my inner child and he is a little brat."

He spit out his pacifier and wrote *Risk* on the wall in crayon.

And I, the man, grabbed the crayon and wrote *Trust* where *Risk* had been before.

I was a child sitting by the tree. My eyes went up the decorations to the peak. I looked out the window to the East. I waited for The Return of the Fullness, to not put me in a tomb, but nestle me back, to the womb.

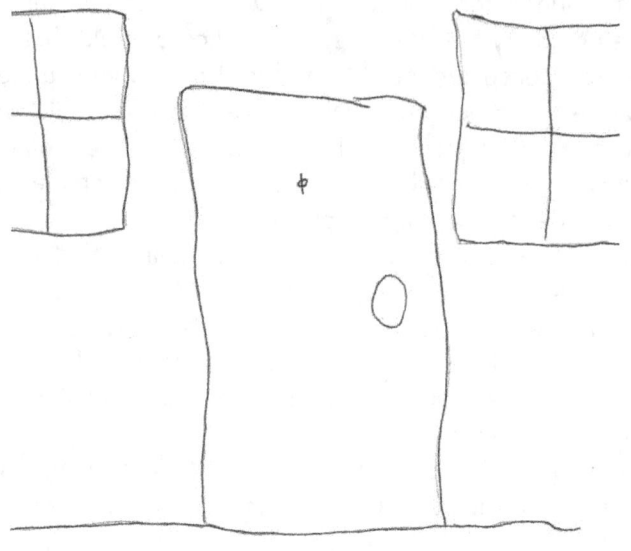

There is a stranger
    at my door.
But have I
    become strange?
As I carry my lantern to meet him
    and look through
    the window
    I don't recognize
    his face.
He continues to
    knock.
And I frantically search my mind.
    I have been left here alone
        all this time.
I look at my fire
    and finally open
        the door.
When he comes
    in we cry and embrace.
        He looks at me
        and says,
                "Welcome Home."

.

HOUND OF THE BASKERVILLES

The smashing of two rams
    A fire in an orchard
The suckling of a lamb

    Love is lava
        bubbling beneath a crater
    It carries the power
    and the gentleness of nature

When you see something beautiful
    look away
not because it is too beautiful
    but out of respect
and not for beauty
    but for the dream
        behind it

    Something beautiful
        grew on a hill
    and beneath
        it lay a soul
    And as it reached
        its head desperately out of the soil
            sending flowers
            fluttering in an array of colors
    it came out
        in a black and white suit
    and whispered, Remember
        Beauty is the enemy of Truth

DODO

60

I'd rather be a stickman
than a vulture.
Better none
than dead culture.

Than Dead Culture, Better
No Culture at All.

Better No Culture at All
than Dead Culture.

Slave worries
and push-pop destiny

manifest in me.
Fire like baptismal water branded me.

Christ brought the dark force
    of pure power,
        called Agrippa, or the feminine.

    Christ carried two forces
        to the cross
           and made them balance.

        And his stardust
          spread colza
              to the four corners of the Earth.

We sat
in the night
with a tentmaker
There were
Jerusalem Crickets
outside
We hummed
a song
for the Children
of the Earth
"Call me nameless
Who is Paul?
Who is Apollos?
All those
struck down on
the road to Damascus
truly know
God you love your people so."

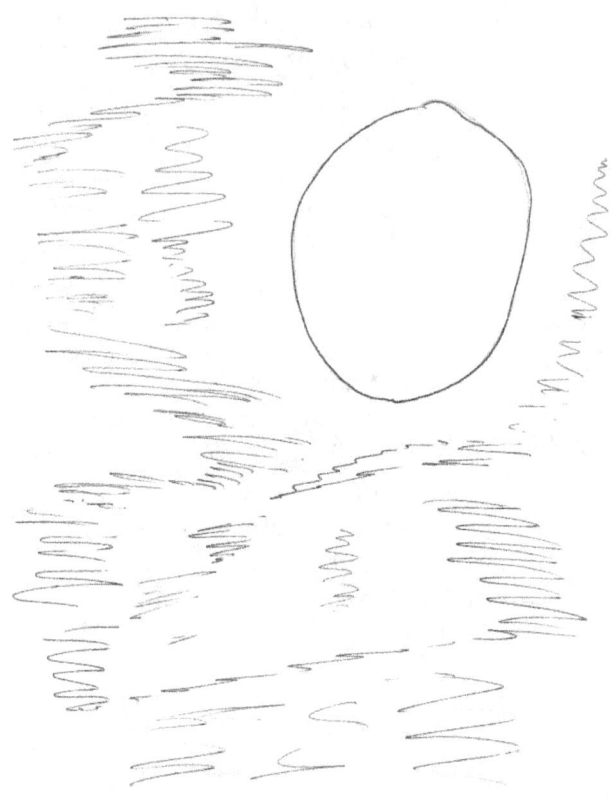

The room grows more
       beautiful by the day
       I know I want to stay
           It has many
           reflective pools
           and there is a moon
           too pure to behold
           with the naked eye

       It's so quiet to be part of the local group

The
Orchard

GUY FAWKES DAY

SWAN
LANDING
IN A LAKE

This Halloween my costume
    was the cat that Superman saved from a tree.
I walked out on our ledge.
    There were shadows beneath but I was confident.
I looked up to the sky to see a sparrow.
    I waited and slept peacefully.

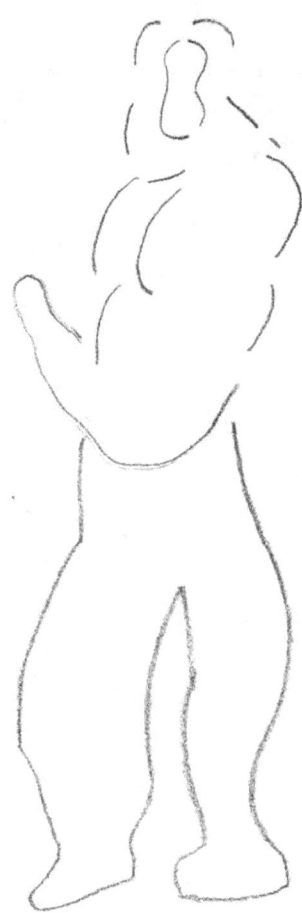

PEANUT
HEAD

I was woken up by my friends
who arrived at my house.
The first friend was dressed in dull gray
with a pole taped to his back that went up above his head.
I asked, "Who or what are you?"
He said, "I'm a lightning rod because the Lord has not deprived
    me of the storm."
My other friend came in in a soft assortment of colors, dim: red,
    green and
yellow. She was covered with lettuce, cabbage and squash
    refuse.
 I asked, "Who or what are you?" She said, "I'm a compost pile,
because the Lord
has grown me despite my refusal to grow."

PEANUT HEAD PUSH-UPS

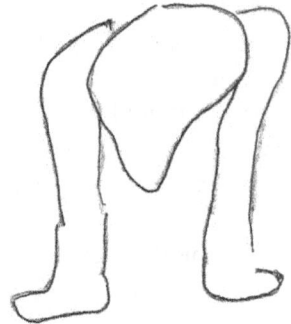

    We walked out into the night
and came across some other kids who were wearing superhero
    costumes.
To the kid in the Superman costume I said,
"I'm the cat you rescued from a tree."
To the girl dressed as Storm from the XMen,
my friend dressed as a lightning rod said,
"I absorb the lightning you make from your eyes so houses
    won't burn."
And to the kid dressed as The Human Torch from the Fantastic
    Four,
my friend who was dressed as a compost pile said,
"I am what grows in the wake of fire and destruction."

LOCAL GADFLY

The other kids in superhero costumes invited us
into their house as they were having a party.
The kid in the Superman costume turned on some music and
asked me,
"Do you like this song?" I listened to the singer of the song,
who was a young woman, and she sang,
"I'm leaving you, you didn't return my calls, so I'm moving on,
my friends think you're crazy."
I asked the kid in the Superman costume,
"The singer of the song, is she talking to me?"
The kid in the Superman costume said,
"No, she's talking to her boyfriend."
So I said, "I don't think it's my place to like or not like the song,
then. It's none of my business."

.

ZILCH

My friends and I left the party and headed toward my house.
It was dark and, suddenly, from behind a tree a kid in a clown
    costume
jumped out at us and shouted, "Ahhh!"
My friend in the lightning rod costume said,
"Are you ok? You seem a little anxious.
It's ok, there's nothing to be anxious about."
The kid in the clown costume said,
"Aren't you scared?"
My friend said, "I have nothing to be scared of."
And the kid in the clown costume said,
"No, it's fun, it's surprising."
My friend in the lightning rod costume said, "I love surprises.
Try it again."
The kid in the clown costume said, "No, it wouldn't be the
    same."
And he walked away. My friend in the compost pile costume
    said,
"It's dark, take our lantern." But the kid in the clown costume
    kept walking away
from us. We shrugged our shoulders and walked home.

.

Swallowing
Camels

I was driven into the Earth's maw
until my nails were like raven's claws
and then, in the sky, a sight I never saw.

There was a soft rill of a sound
   that was like a pang.
I looked at my hands covered in mud,
   my eyes fresh from tears.
      The air was new.

I felt like a son who
had just been corrected by a loving father.
As I looked up I felt loved.
The air was crisp
and the stars were so pure.

In the mud,
I saw a banner that I had cast from the castle.
  It was strewn on the ground, brown with mud.
I held it up and saw the royal insignia.
    I had wanted to be the one king, above this crest.
        I picked it up and wept.

I got to the castle and a servant met me at the door.
He bowed at my feet.
I reached down and picked him up by the arm and told him,
"Don't cower or appease, you are here to serve and not to
    please."
I saluted him and thanked him for his service.
I went to the upper room of the castle,
reached out to the flag pole,
and raised the fallen banner.

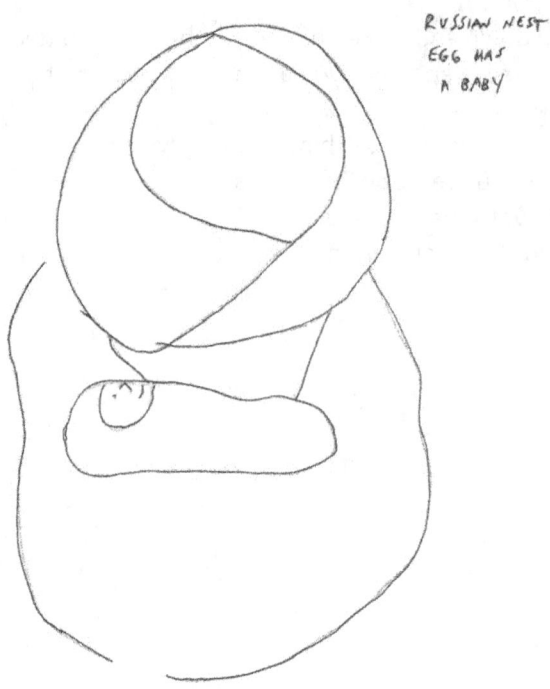

RUSSIAN NEST
EGG HAS
A BABY

I've seen the tree that looked like Dimestore
Philosophy, New Swine and a dark sunset that
led me to
    a sign that said, *Bat Meat*.

The trees this twilight were flooded with moth-like
birds that moved like bats. The fluttering betwixt the
moss hives high in the amber was enough to drive you
to tears. Why do the trees stand still?

IDLE PRENTICE
READS
BASHO

I stared at
  the fence
  and shouted,
   "Seeds belong
  in the ground."
There was a
    gale in the
    clouds and
    mist in the dark
    I said,
        "It was as much
        the wind as the sky."

IDLE PRENTICE LEADS AN ORCHESTRA

Seeds are swept up in the sky.
The wind funnels them past the storm siren,
and back down into the barn,
where their horses have scattered
and leaves fly, swirling down where they belong.
They spin past the single remaining foal,
and swirl down into the whole.

Rhino Zygotes

The men returned
to their Master and said,
"We have done as you have told us to do
and we fed the blind man at the gate."
The Master said,
"I would that there would be adventure between meals."

The blind man was blinded by the sun
and saw a distant tire swing.
There was an orchard.
The blind man cried
as this was the most beautiful thing he had ever seen.

The blind man ran through a meadow
and there were flowers that flowed and green.
The sky turned a purple shade of red.
He saw dragons in the sky.
There was ice in the river.
With fire, the dragons melted the ice the man was standing on
and the man sank into the water.
The water was aquamarine and there were fish dreaming.

.

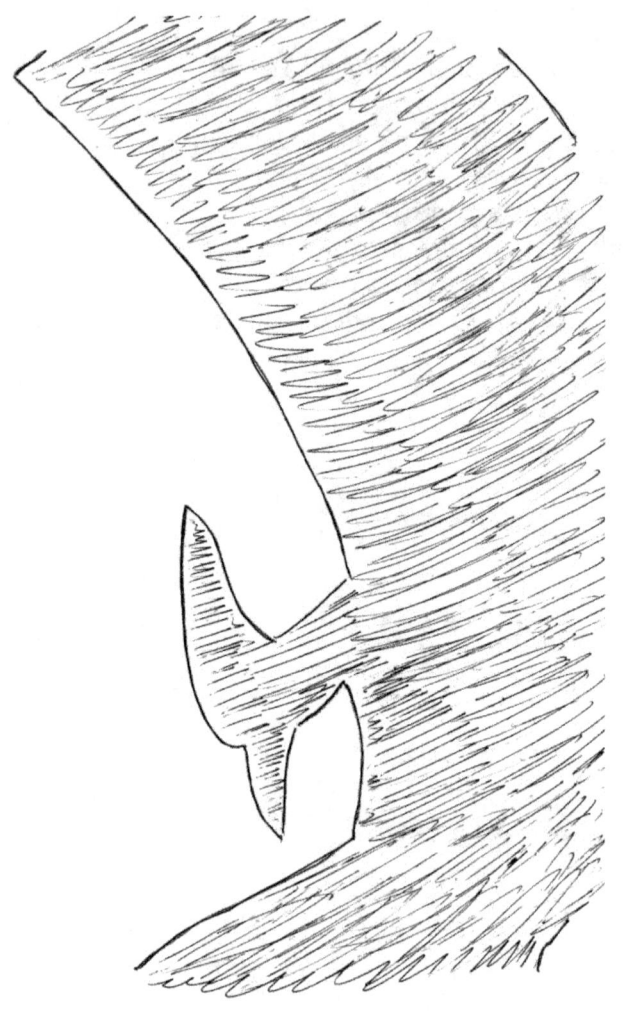

The man remembered warm feelings
of red and yellow in this green.
The river was vast.
It had underwater buildings and a white-lit sky.
The fish told him to use the water to destroy the dragon.
This man drifted to the surface in the lily pads.
He rested on the calm waters and dreamed.

The Dragon came back
and shot warm fire near the man.
The man warmed his fingers in the wake of the smoke.
Then he saw the dragon's red eyes
come through the smoke right toward him.
The man swirled in the water
and splashed water into the nostrils of the dragon
and watched the dragon fall to the sea.
The man heard the clang of the cup he was begging with
as he calmly tapped the lid.

Deena Letter

I want to tell a beautiful story. I have a friend named Deena.

Deena makes collages of Disney characters and how they relate to her life, the trials and adversities that the Lord Jesus overcomes in her life. She was at Disneyland in the process of living out a collage of a certain character when the Lord spoke to her. She was on the ride, *It's a Small World*, and the Lord told her to forget the character she was making a collage of and make a collage of Aladdin. The Lord placed the song *A Whole New World* in her mind, the song where Aladdin takes his woman love on a magic carpet ride and shows her the world. Deena told me that at first she thought that a man would come into her life that would show her a whole new world, but then she realized, no, it was God who wanted to take her on a ride of wonders if she would go.

About a week later Deena and I went to the Disney *Princess on Ice* show. Deena wanted to see the *Aladdin* performance most of all.

We stopped at a restaurant before the show and were kind of pressed for time. The waitress was in her thirties and had a princess crown. The waitress told Deena, "I told my girlfriend I had to wear this. The Princesses are in town." Deena thought this was cool and funny, as did I. Deena has such an openess to the Lord's connections with people. We were joking that "The Princesses are in town" on the way to the show. We were running late and had problems with parking. I didn't have enough cash so I had to use the ATM at the gas station. I was worried we would miss the *Aladdin* performance. We parked and went to Will Call to get our tickets. There was a little bit of a line. We walked in the arena and it was dark. And as we were standing at the railing of the dark arena, the lights came on, the song could be heard, *A Whole New World*, and at that time the Aladdin character came out and took Jasmine away on a magic carpet. As Deena stood there crying, I could only think "God is Good." The Lord got us there at exactly the right moment. We were both overwhelmed. We went to our seats and enjoyed the rest of the show.

A couple weeks later I talked to Deena. She told me that she would not be attending Thanksgiving with her family, her parents and sister and the rest of the family. Instead, she would have Thanksgiving in her apartment. By herself—in a way. She was going to set her table with two settings: one setting for her and one for God.

A week later I received a call. It was from my boss. He told me that Deena was driving her scooter to work when she lost control, hit a car, then a pole, and passed away. I was in shock, and am to this day. At first I wanted to pray for Deena. But how could I pray for a saved person? Jesus paid all the cost for Deena already. I cannot add or take away from this work. He saved her infinitely. How could I possibly do anything to add or detract from this? Deena is in His hands and as the Bible says, "My Father is stronger than I and no man can pluck them from His hand."

I was very sad when I heard this news. But I gave it to God and God gave me this poem.

The Lord Is a Miracle Worker.

THE SEPARATION

Her family was upset that she wasn't
coming over for Thanksgiving.
She said, "I will dine at my table.
I will place two settings.
One place will be for me,
one place will be empty
and the empty place is for God."
And it was like God said,
"I like your table
and your china is fine,
but I've got a better idea.
Let's eat at mine."

Tonight I worked as a job coach in a grocery store, a Vons, just like the Vons where Deena worked. I was her job coach for a few months and while there, Deena and I became friends. Tonight, the man I was working with as a new bagger, did well. I noticed there was a kid begging next to us that reminded me of a guy that worked at Deena's store. The baggers tonight had to say to the checkers, "Bob," which means "Bottom of basket," if they had waters or something on the bottom tray of the cart. Deena had a manager that used to grind this. "Hey Deena, did you ask about Bob? How about that Bob?" She said he used to say this five times a minute to her. We joked that we should get this manager the movie *What About Bob?* for his birthday. I was thinking about this tonight and laughing when I looked up and in the line checking out at my guy's line was Richard Dreyfuss. The man I was working with said, "I think I know him." I laughed and said, "I know." And my guy said, "I think he was in the movie *What About Bob?*" I laughed as we had not talked about this at all before this. He didn't know Deena. We carried his groceries to his car and he tried to tip us. We laughed and said we couldn't accept tips. He said, "In this economy?" I laughed and had a moment with Deena. We got inside and my guy said, "He was a famous actor." I said, "Yeah, he's been in a lot of movies. He was in *Jaws*." And my guy corrected me and said, "No, he was in *What About Bob?*"

"I was a child when I had my first vision. My sister Abbie was wearing a familiar skirt. She had just died and I didn't know it then. She lifted into the air and I cried, "Abbie, Abbie."
— Reverend Howard Finster

My cousin Mary Beth had a pregnancy
with a boy child.
Her two-year-old son would listen to her stomach
and say, "Abbie."
The pregnancy had complications and we weren't sure
If the baby would make it.
Between then, my friend Deena passed away.
I had a vision of Deena in her glorified body.
As she glorified Jesus Christ who had saved her,
my soul could only utter, "She wore a familiar skirt."
And my cousin continued to struggle
with her pregnancy.
The baby came one day at 7:00 a.m., exactly,
and weighed 9 pounds, 3 ounces.
I went and saw baby Garrett
and I looked in his eyes
with mine crying:
"Abbie."

Acknowledgments

Many of the poems in this book were first published in *The Penwood Review*.

Credits

Cover: *Earth, Sun, Space*
Image by GooKingSword
Pixabay.com

front cover concept: Ashley Farrand

Interior Art:

drawings by Andy Palasciano

Interior Design: Isabel Williams

Cover Design: Walt Dakin

Also by the same author

The Warrior: Tales of a Substitute Teacher and Job Coach
(Lymer & Hart: 2019)

About the Author

Andy Palasciano was born in Connecticut and spent his childhood there before moving to the Inland Empire near L.A., where he went to high school. He graduated from San Diego State University with a degree in English Literature. He became part of the Full Moon Poetry Circle in San Diego's North County.

His work has appeared in the *San Diego Poetry Annual, The Penwood Review, The Union Tribune, Knot Literary Review, Poets Underground (Volume One)*, and other publications.

His memoir is *The Warrior: Tales of a Substitute Teacher and Job Coach* (Lymer & Hart: 2019).